KU-453-012

The Best Den Ever

First published in 2004 by
Franklin Watts
96 Leonard Street
London
EC2A 4XD

Franklin Watts Australia
45–51 Huntley Street
Alexandria
NSW 2015

Text © Anne Cassidy 2004
Illustration © Deborah Allwright 2004

A CIP catalogue record for this book is available
from the British Library.

ISBN 0 7496 5872 X (hbk)
ISBN 0 7496 5876 2 (pbk)

Series Editor: Jackie Hamley
Series Advisor: Dr Barrie Wade
Cover Design: Jason Anscomb
Design: Peter Scoulding

Printed in Hong Kong / China

The Best Den Ever

by Anne Cassidy and Deborah Allwright

W

FRANKLIN WATTS
LONDON • SYDNEY

Sam wanted to build a den.

His sister Sophie wanted to help.

"Let's build our den in the garden,"
said Sam. He got some deck chairs
and an umbrella.

"We can use these sheets," he said.
Sam and Sophie made a den
under the deck chairs.

Inside the den, Sam put cushions, toys and a chair for Sophie.

Sam's brother, Joe, came to see it.
"Look!" cried Sam. "We've finished
building our den!"

"This is the worst den ever," said Joe. "It'll fall down! Look at those silly sheets and shaky deck chairs!" "They're OK!" said Sam.

Sam tied the sheets tighter and
fixed the deck chairs.
"Well, the umbrella is full
of holes!" said Joe.

Later it rained. The umbrella leaked. The deck chairs got soaked. The sheets fell down.

"Oh no!" cried Sam. He picked up
the cushions and ran. Sophie
pulled her teddy bear behind her.

When the sun came out,
Sam tried again. "This time
we'll build our den under
this tree," he said.
"And this time it
won't fall down!"

Sophie helped to make a pile of bricks. Sam fetched some wood.

On the top they laid some towels.

"That's much better!" said Sam.

Inside the den, Sam put a chair, a table, some cups, a tray with biscuits and a drink for Sophie.

"I could build a much better den," said Joe. "And it wouldn't fall over!"

"This den won't fall over!" said Sam.

But later it was windy. The towels blew away. The wood fell over.

"Quick! Let's go!" said Sam.

"I told you it would fall over!"

said Joe, laughing.

"We need to find a better place
to build our den," said Sam.
They looked around.

Sophie's room was too small.

Sam's room was too messy!

Sam and Sophie looked everywhere.

The kitchen was too full.

The living room was too tidy.

The hallway was too empty.

Suddenly Sam had an idea.

"I know a good place!"

he whispered to Sophie.

Sam got some pillows and blankets.

He found a chair and a stool.

Sophie brought toys from her room.

They made the best den ever ...

... in Joe's room!

"WHAT'S THIS?" demanded Joe.

"It's the best den ever!" said Sam.

"Well, I suppose it's not too bad!"

laughed Joe.

Hopscotch has been specially designed to fit the requirements of the National Literacy Strategy. It offers real books by top authors and illustrators for children developing their reading skills.

There are 25 Hopscotch stories to choose from:

Marvin, the Blue Pig
Written by Karen Wallace
Illustrated by Lisa Williams

Plip and Plop
Written by Penny Dolan
Illustrated by Lisa Smith

The Queen's Dragon
Written by Anne Cassidy
Illustrated by Gwyneth Williamson

Flora McQuack
Written by Penny Dolan
Illustrated by Kay Widdowson

Willie the Whale
Written by Joy Oades
Illustrated by Barbara Vagnozzi

Naughty Nancy
Written by Anne Cassidy
Illustrated by Desideria Guicciardini

Run!
Written by Sue Ferraby
Illustrated by Fabiano Fiorin

The Playground Snake
Written by Brian Moses
Illustrated by David Mostyn

"Sausages!"
Written by Anne Adeney
Illustrated by Roger Fereday

The Truth about Hansel and Gretel
Written by Karina Law
Illustrated by Elke Counsell

Pippin's Big Jump
Written by Hilary Robinson
Illustrated by Sarah Warburton

Whose Birthday Is It?
Written by Sherryl Clark
Illustrated by Jan Smith

The Princess and the Frog
Written by Margaret Nash
Illustrated by Martin Remphry

Flynn Flies High
Written by Hilary Robinson
Illustrated by Tim Archbold

Clever Cat
Written by Karen Wallace
Illustrated by Anni Axworthy

Moo!
Written by Penny Dolan
Illustrated by Melanie Sharp

Izzie's Idea
Written by Jillian Powell
Illustrated by Leonie Shearing

Roly-poly Rice Ball
Written by Penny Dolan
Illustrated by Diana Mayo

I Can't Stand It!
Written by Anne Adeney
Illustrated by Mike Phillips

Cockerel's Big Egg
Written by Damian Harvey
Illustrated by François Hall

The Truth about those Billy Goats
Written by Karina Law
Illustrated by Graham Philpot

Bear in Town
Written by A. H. Benjamin
Illustrated by Richard Watson

Marlowe's Mum and the Tree House
Written by Karina Law
Illustrated by Ross Collins

The Best Den Ever
Written by Anne Cassidy
Illustrated by Deborah Allwright

How to Teach a Dragon Manners
Written by Hilary Robinson
Illustrated by Jane Abbott